Two for Stew

To Ace, Lily, Susan, and
Barney, with love
—L.N.

For Anita and Bill, two who
knew a good bowl of stew
—B.S.

To my wife, Nancy
—S.M.

Two for Stew

by Laura Numeroff *and* Barney Saltzberg

illustrated by

Salvatore Murdocca

Simon & Schuster Books For Young Readers

Good evening, Madame.
And how do you do?
I'd like a table,
A table for two.

I'll bring you a menu
In a minute or two.
No need to bother.
We came for the stew.

There is no more stew,
I'm sorry to say.
We do have some noodles,
Will that be okay?

No, thank you, kind sir,
We never touch noodles.
They're messy to eat,
And not fit for poodles.

I think you'd enjoy
Our ham nuggets and peas.
Oh, no, thank you, sir,
Two bowls of stew, please.

Look through the menu,
Won't something else do?
But we had our hearts set
On your world-famous stew.

There's nothing quite like it—
It's chunky, yet creamy.
It tickles our taste buds,
It's ever so dreamy.

WONDERFUL STEW

I'm really quite sorry,
We're all out of stew.
A busload of tourists
From Spain just came through.

They ate every drop—
Oh, what could I do?
Had I known you were coming,
I'd have saved some for you.

The special tonight
Is a wonderful dish.
Oh, please won't you try
Our gravy and fish?

Fish makes me seasick
And gives him a rash.
The last batch we had
Went right in the trash.

Can't your chef make some?
Oh, please don't say no.
We must taste your stew—
One bite and we'll go.

The chef's not the one
Who makes it, you see.
My grandmother does,
From an old recipe.

That's why it's so great!
We just never knew.
Can we go to her house
And ask for some stew?

I guess we can go.
My bike's right outside.
Hop in, grab a helmet.
I'll give you a ride.

I've never brought guests
To Grandma's before . . .
Won't she be surprised
When she opens the door!

She's a wonderful cook.
She bakes a mean strudel.
Maybe she'll make some
For me and my poodle!

Uh-oh, there goes Grandma
In that car at the light.
I forgot that it's Tuesday,
Her big bowling night.

You can't mean it. Bowling?
Then it's no stew for us?
I've been trying to tell you,
But you made such a fuss.

Well, there is one more thing,
One thing you can do:

SIMON & SCHUSTER BOOKS FOR YOUNG READERS
An imprint of Simon & Schuster Children's Publishing Division
1230 Avenue of the Americas, New York, New York 10020
Copyright © 1996 by Laura Numeroff and Barney Saltzberg
Illustrations copyright © 1996 by Salvatore Murdocca

SIMON & SCHUSTER BOOKS FOR YOUNG READERS is a trademark of Simon & Schuster.

Book design by Anahid Hamparian
The text for this book is set in 22-point Bernhard Fashion and 16-point Caslon 224 ITC
The illustrations are rendered in ink, watercolor, and colored pencil
Printed and bound in the United States of America
First Edition
10 9 8 7 6 5 4 3 2 1

Library of Congress Cataloging-in-Publication Data
Numeroff, Laura Joffe.
Two for stew / Laura Numeroff and Barney Saltzberg : illustrated by Sal Murdocca. — 1st ed.
p.   cm.
Summary: Because the restaurant has no more stew, and the grandmother who makes it is out for
the evening, two friends find a different way to enjoy themselves.
[1. Dinners and dining—Fiction. 2. Food—Fiction. 3. Grandmothers—Fiction. 4. Stories in
rhyme.] I. Saltzberg, Barney. II. Murdocca, Sal, ill. III. Title.
PZ8.3.N92Tw 1996
[E]—dc20 95-45744
ISBN 0-689-80571-3